The Mysterious Old Church

The Mysterious Old Church

Neil S. Wilson

Tyndale House Publishers, Inc.
Wheaton, Illinois

Books in the Choice Adventures series

Cover illustration copyright © 1991 by Wendy Wassink
Library of Congress Catalog Card Number 90-71869
ISBN 0-8423-5025-X
Copyright © 1991 by The Livingstone Corporation
All rights reserved
Printed in the United States of America
99 98 97 96 95 94
9 8 7

"**S**ummer vacation should never start on Saturday!" said Willy as he leaned back on the old stone steps and soaked up the sun. The day before had been the last day of the school year.

"Yeah, I know," said Chris. "It just doesn't feel like summer till you get to sleep in on a week day. Don't call me on Monday morning, Willy, or you'll be in big trouble! I'm gonna stay in bed till at least ten."

Willy laughed. "What are you gonna do? Dream up some plans for this summer?"

Chris moved sideways until he was blocking the late morning sun Willy was enjoying. "Well, my first plan is to stay as far away from Madison Junior High as I can," he said.

"Hey, get out of my sun!" yelled Willy in fake anger. "I gotta work on my tan." He smiled as he tilted his black face toward the sky.

Chris realized what a great friend Willy was, but he didn't think he could ever say it. Instead, he sat down beside him and pushed him away, saying, "You think you need a tan? Look at this work of art!" He pulled up his shorts leg where there was already a red sunburn line on the white skin.

The two boys had known each other since fourth grade, when Willy and his parents had moved into the apartment above the one Chris and his mom lived in. Whenever Willy was in trouble, his mother called him William George Washington, which was his real name. Chris's name was Christopher James Martin. Kids at school sometimes called them Salt and Pepper because they were always doing something together. If this summer turned out like the last ones, there would be plenty of adventure for them and their friends.

They both laid back on the stairs. The smooth, worn steps were cold and hard, so they put their hands under their heads as they looked up. Above them, the sky was bright blue, which made the tower of the old white building behind them shine in the sun. It was a church. They had heard it was one of the oldest buildings in the Washington, D.C., area. It had been built before the Revolutionary War. That meant the church was almost 250 years old. The last paint job on the church was beginning to crack and peel. The building needed help.

In fact, both boys had gone to the church often with their families when Willy first moved to town. There weren't many people attending, and the boys noticed they all seemed sad, like they had lost something very important and couldn't find it. The only person who wasn't sad was Miss Whitehead, their Sunday school teacher. She was old, but she acted young. And she always had a smile and had a twinkle in her eye. She told wonderful stories. The boys knew she hadn't lost what everybody else seemed to be looking for. Then one Sunday she didn't show up for class. Someone came down and told the kids that Miss Whitehead had gone to bed the night before and had died in her sleep. After that, the boys and their parents had looked for another church. But they hadn't found any church where they felt at home. And the boys agreed they hadn't found another Miss Whitehead, either. The old church had been closed for at least a year—locked up tight with no one around.

Willy and Chris had been silent for a while, each thinking his own thoughts. Suddenly, the bell up in the steeple gave a short, clear ring. The boys sat up and looked at each other. There was no wind. As if someone else was controlling their bodies, they both turned at the same time and looked behind them. They hadn't noticed until then that the front door of the church was slightly open. Someone was in the church! They looked back at each other, whispering, at the same time, "What should we do?"

CHOICE ⟹

If you think they should go directly into the building, turn to page 9.

If you think they should gather some other friends, then check out the building, turn to page 15.

If you think they should go to the nearby phone booth and dial 911, turn to page 21.

8

Hold everything! Do you seriously think two adventure-minded young men like Willy and Chris would actually leave at a moment like this? Of course not!

Well, you can't leave either.

CHOICE

Please turn to page 73 to stay with them.

Willy and Chris climbed the stone steps slowly and crossed the porch. They could see through the crack where the door was slightly open that the front hallway of the church was dark. Chris grabbed the big brass handle and pulled on the door. It was heavy and creaked softly as it moved toward them. When there was just enough room to let them in, they looked at each other again.

"You sure you want to do this?" asked Chris.

"Are you?" answered Willy with another question.

"I asked first!" said Chris.

"All right," said Willy. "I'm ready if you're ready."

They slipped into the front hallway of the church. The first thing they noticed was that dry, musty smell a building gets when it's been closed up for a long time. As their eyes got used to the dim light, they could see that thick dust covered everything. There was a small window above the door they had just entered, and the light coming through it created long ribbons of dust that floated in the air. The boys passed their hands through the light beams several times to watch the dust swirl. Then they began to notice other interesting things in the room.

Willy whispered as he pointed in the dimness, "Remember those doors, Chris?"

In front of them was another pair of thick carved doors leading into the main part of the church. Willy stared at the large lion and lamb that had been carved on those doors. They were wood colored, but seemed very real. The animals had been carved in such a way that their heads almost met at the crack between the two doors. But their faces were turned so that anyone opening the doors had to look into their eyes. Both animals seemed to be ready to step out of the doors and into the foyer of the church. Several times when the church was still open, Willy had been sure the two animals were watching him as he passed by them into the worship service with his parents. He had always wondered what they would feel like. He walked over to touch the lion carving, but changed his mind and put his hand on the wooden wool of the lamb on the other door instead. It was so lifelike that he expected his hand to sink into the wool along the lamb's back. A moment later, when he touched the lamb's ear, he thought he felt it move slightly. Then there was a click behind him, and suddenly a hidden door in the wall on their right swung open. Willy jumped back in surprise.

Chris had followed Willy to the doors and was almost knocked down by Willy's jump. "Would you warn me before you do that?!" he whispered loudly.

Together, the boys shuffled slowly toward the new doorway. They could see a narrow stairway leading up. Somewhere above, there was a dim light. They looked at each other, wondering what to do next. Chris saw something and pointed down at the stairs. On each of the steps they could see a very clear footprint in the thick dust. Whoever was in the church had gone up those stairs.

Willy swallowed hard. He wanted to run. But he was

also very curious about what might be going on in the old church.

If you think Willy and Chris should follow the footprints up the stairs, turn to page 23.

If you think Willy and Chris should call loudly for the mysterious visitor, turn to page 30.

12

"I'm sorry, Mrs. Whitehead, I thought for sure we would find the boys at the Freeze. I just can't imagine where they could be." Chris recognized one of the voices before two women got through the thick evergreens. An elderly woman with silver hair and a wise smile pushed her way through the branches followed closely by somebody the boys all knew. It was Chris's mother. She spotted them almost instantly. "Well, look who's here! We've been trying to find you boys all over town. We could really use your help around here."

Sam chuckled and mumbled under his breath, "Sounds like work to me."

Chris said, "Mom . . ." He was trying to think of an important appointment, an allergy, or some other reason to leave immediately, but his mind went blank.

His mother continued, "I told Mrs. Whitehead I knew several boys who would be glad to whack down a few weeds, and make this backyard presentable. But first let me introduce you to her." She pointed at each boy in turn as she said, "Mrs. Whitehead, I'd like you to meet my boy Chris and his three best friends: Willy, Sam, and Pete. Boys, this is Mrs. Whitehead, wife of the new pastor of the church."

They all mumbled something that sounded like, "Pleased to meet you."

Mrs. Whitehead gave them a friendly smile and said, "Nice to meet you boys. There's someone else around here I really want you to meet." She disappeared into the church and they heard her faintly calling, "Jim! J-i-i-im! Would you come out back for a while?" Moments later she appeared again, this time with a boy about their age behind her. He was covered in dust.

Sometimes getting dirty is very unpleasant; other times it's the best of fun. From the look in Jim's eyes, Chris guessed he had been having a great time somewhere. Jim was introduced as Mrs. Whitehead's grandson. Then they were all put to weed work.

Between bursts of chopping, weed tossing, rest stops, lemonade, and the unavoidable bumping, pushing, and wrestling that tends to break out whenever junior high boys work together, the yard actually did begin to look better. And the boys got to know Jim a little. They discovered he had just moved from Brazil, that his favorite sport was soccer, and that he would be living with his grandparents in Millersburg because his parents were missionaries in Brazil.

Chris finally got around to asking him how he got so dirty in the church. Jim's eyes twinkled, and he smiled. "You guys are not going to believe what I found in this church. I'll have to take you on a tour sometime. All I can promise you is a real adventure."

In the meantime, though, the boys had a full afternoon's weeds surrounding them. Sometimes adventures have to wait until the work is done.

14

THE END
Turn to page 125.

"**C**ome on," said Chris in a hard whisper, "let's go find Sam and Pete!" He stood up and began running down Main Street. Willy was right on his heels. They turned the corner at Oak Street, travelled one block, and then turned left on Pine Street. As they flew around the corner, they almost ran into two boys their own age.

"Hey, we were just coming to find you guys," said Sam, a short boy with bronze skin and a wide smile.

"So were we!" answered Chris. "Want to come with us and check out something strange?"

Pete, who was taller and thinner than any of them, spoke up. "Summer's hardly started and you guys have already found something strange? What is it?"

"Somebody's in the old church!" exclaimed Willy.

"How do you know that?" asked Pete. He was a hard one to convince.

Chris was ready with an answer. "We heard the bell ring like someone was messing with it, and then we saw that the door was open, just a little."

"Maybe it's just one of the old members doing some cleaning," said Pete.

Sam said, "I don't think so. They said at my church that the people gave up on that church and closed it for good. I say we check it out."

Even though Pete wasn't all that excited about the

idea, they started back the way Chris and Willy had just come.

Besides sleeping in on a week day, adventures are what make summer a lot of fun. The boys could just see the steeple of the church sticking above the buildings on Oak Street as they walked toward the Common. Millersburg had a large park with trees and grass right in the middle of town. The kids in Millersburg spent most of their free time at the Common. During the long summer evenings they played endless games of capture the flag. On this sunny day, however, the park was empty. Most people were at work or home for lunch. But, somehow, boys on the way to an adventure always manage to forget it's almost lunch time.

As they turned the corner onto Main Street, Sam suddenly took off running. "Last one there buys the pop!" he shouted over his shoulder. The other three were immediately in hot pursuit, laughing and bumping into each other. Sam took advantage of his early start and beat them to the church steps. He ran up them two at a time and tried the door. It was locked.

He turned as the others ran up and said, "I thought you told us the door was open."

"It was just a few minutes ago," huffed Willy. Sometimes challenges made him forget his asthma. He pulled out his inhaler and took a deep breath through it.

"Well, it isn't open now," said Sam.

Pete chimed in, "Listen, did you guys really hear or see anything? Are you just trying to trick us?"

Sometimes Chris got a little impatient with Pete. This

was one of those times. "Look, Pete," he said, "Willy and me both heard the bell. And the door was really open."

"Young man," said Sam, imitating one of their teachers, "I'm ashamed of you. Less than a day out of school and your English is falling apart. It's 'Willy and I,' not 'Willy and me.' One more slipup and it's summer school for you!" He was laughing before he finished, and Willy joined him.

Meanwhile, Pete and Chris were just looking at each other like people do when they are trying to decide whether or not to get angry. Both Sam and Willy stopped laughing.

After a few moments, Chris suggested they go around and check the back door of the church. Pete shook his head and said, "It's just a waste of time. Let's go over to the Freeze and get something to drink." Things had gotten a little tense.

CHOICE ⇒

If you think Chris should try to convince Pete to stay with them and check out the church, turn to page 26.

If you think Pete should go off on his own, turn to page 40.

If you think Sam or Willy should help Pete and Chris agree, turn to page 34.

18

Before the boys could think what to do, the door on their right flew open and a hand reached out and yanked Willy inside. At the same time they heard a whisper, "In here!" The rest followed immediately. The door closed to a crack, and there was silence in the darkness.

They heard footsteps in the hallway, and Dave Brown's voice saying, "It was just a bucket that fell off the landing. Listen, Mayor, I really need to be on my way. You coming with me?"

The mayor said something to Mrs. Whitehead that the boys couldn't hear, then the two men walked past the door and out the back.

"Man, that was close!" whispered an unfamiliar voice.

"I think 'surprised out of my socks' puts it a little better," said Sam. "Who are you, anyway?"

Pete found the light switch and turned it on, saying, "And why did you pull us in here? We weren't doing anything wrong."

The light revealed a boy their own age, with black hair and a tan as deep as Sam's natural skin. The boy chuckled and said, "I saw you guys hiding out in the weeds, and I wanted to meet you, so I thought I would help you hide again. Say, do you guys sneak around a lot like this?"

It was Sam's turn. "No, we're just making this up as we go along," he said, laughing softly.

Looking around the room, the boys noticed a long table, set with four plates. Along one wall of the room was a kitchen area with a sink, small refrigerator, and a stove. On the stove were several pots steaming with strange but wonderful smells that reminded the boys they had missed lunch.

The new boy seemed to read their minds. "You guys want to eat with us?" He opened the door and called out, "Grandma, can I invite four more to lunch?" Then he turned around and said, "By the way, my name is Jim."

There were footsteps in the hall as each boy introduced himself. Mrs. Whitehead bustled into the room and announced, "You boys are in luck. We always fix a big pot in Brazil." She walked over to the stove to stir one of the pots. As she lifted the cover, a mouth-watering aroma filled the room.

"If you boys will all wash your hands," she added, "we can eat. Jim, your grandfather and sister had to leave on errands for the afternoon, so it's nice to have company."

As they sat at the table, the woman asked Jim to give thanks for the food. They all bowed their heads and Jim said a simple prayer. Then they began to eat. The boys agreed later they had never tasted better food. Their plates were covered with a chicken-flavored rice, then heaped high with a black bean stew. They also agreed that if the food was that good in Brazil, it might be a good reason to visit there sometime.

20

During the meal, Mrs. Whitehead asked Jim, "So, where did you meet these boys?"

The boys looked at each other and chuckled. "I just kind of found them hanging around here, Grandma," said Jim.

"Well, I hope they hang around a lot more in the future," said Mrs. Whitehead. She couldn't have known how much her hope would come true. The five boys she was feeding would become part of the Ringers of Millersburg.

THE END

For other adventures, turn back to the beginning and make different choices, or turn to page 125.

Chris and Willy dashed to the phone booth that stood on the corner. Willy picked up the receiver and quickly dialed 911. He heard a voice on the line say, "Deposit twenty-five cents, please."

Willy turned to Chris. "You got a quarter?"

Chris pulled out his only coin and handed it over. Willy tried again. This time, the line went dead. He pulled on the receiver hook several times. The only result was the sound of Chris's last quarter falling into the holding box of the telephone.

Willy hung up the phone and turned to his friend. "I've got some bad news and some worse news, Chris. The phone doesn't work, and it ate your quarter for dessert."

"Now what do we do?" asked Chris.

CHOICE ⇒

You didn't really think calling 911 was that great an idea anyway, did you? Turn back to page 7 and make another choice.

"**W**e'll surprise them when we catch up with them in the dark," said Sam with a chuckle, and he began sliding down the stairs. Willy followed.

Soon, Sam decided he would stand up. He knew there were many steps to go down, and he wasn't very excited about doing it in the sitting position. He felt a stone block that was sticking out of the wall a little, so he used it to lift himself. As he did, the block he was pulling on moved ever so slightly and a sliding noise began behind them.

"Oh, oh," said Sam.

"You got that right, Sam," whispered Willy harshly. "The door just closed. Pete and Chris are not going to be pleased. I'm not all that pleased either! Now what do we do?"

CHOICE ⇒

If you think Sam and Willy should continue with their plan to catch up with Pete and Chris, turn to page 62.

If you think Sam and Willy should try to find a way to open the door, turn to page 86.

The stairs were too narrow for Willy and Chris to climb them side by side. But they tried anyway. The steep stairway made a sharp left-hand turn, passed by another small window, and disappeared into the darkness. Chris checked the wall for a light switch. Nothing. He said to Willy, "You got a flashlight?"

"Who do you think I am, Indiana Jones?" answered Willy.

As they crept up into the darkness, they began to hear a very soft noise. They stopped to listen. The noise stopped, too. They waited for a moment, then began to move again. The noise started again, but this time it was a quiet whistling, and it seemed a long way off.

Chris lifted his foot to take another step and walked right into a wall. "Huh," he grunted.

Willy whispered from below, "What happened?"

"I ran out of stairs!" answered Chris. His hands flew out in both directions. The right one hit another wall, hard. The left one found only space. The stairs had another sharp turn. "Turning left again," he whispered.

Two more steps and "Huh," he said again. Another wall. Only this one felt different. Of course, it was a door. He felt for the handle and turned it slowly. The door began to open away from them, and the whistling suddenly got louder.

They found themselves in a long, narrow room. In the middle of the room was a small table with a lit candle in a candleholder on it. The flame was flickering in the draft created when the boys opened the door. Next to the table was a ladder disappearing into an opening in the ceiling. The walls of the room were lined with old chairs. There were also many paintings or photographs hanging around the room. Chris and Willy stood there for a moment taking it all in.

The whistling stopped. It was so quiet, Willy thought he could hear Chris's heart beating. Then he realized it was his own heart that he was hearing.

A voice began to sing a song that the boys thought they recognized. The music was coming from the hole in the ceiling, but the words were in a different language:

Em Jesus amigo temos, mais chegado que um irmao,
E nos pede que levemos, tudo a Deus em oracao—

Just then, a foot appeared in the opening and someone began to climb down the ladder. Willy and Chris looked at each other in a panic.

CHOICE ⇒

If you think the boys should try to hide quickly, turn to page 54.

If you think the boys should wait where they are and introduce themselves to this person, turn to page 48.

Chris shrugged his shoulders. "All right," he said slowly, "I guess maybe we've had enough excitement for one day. Let's go."

Pete suddenly felt very foolish. He knew he had spoken up too fast. Deep down, he didn't want to leave. Now his friends were having to give up an adventure for him. He didn't know what to say. Trying to make things right, he said, "Let's head over to the Freeze. I'll buy."

The boys got up quietly and walked out to the alley through the same passageway the policeman and the mayor had used. Friendship isn't always easy.

As it turned out, it wasn't a completely wasted afternoon. At the Freeze they ran into some other boys on their way to play baseball. That kept them busy until supper time.

It wasn't until the following week that they really began their adventures in the old church.

THE END
Turn to page 125.

26

Chris took a deep breath. He had learned that it helped sometimes to keep him from getting angry. Then he said, "You're probably right, Pete. It may be a waste of time. But it will only take a few minutes to check around back. And besides, think how much better that drink at the Freeze will taste after you're a little thirstier."

Pete still looked a little doubtful.

"I'll buy," said Chris with a smile.

That did it. Pete shrugged his shoulders and said, "OK, I guess it won't hurt to waste a little of my summer on this wild chase."

They had just started down the porch steps of the church when the bell suddenly rang again. Four heads looked up in unison, and four bodies almost ended up in a heap at the bottom of the steps. They managed to stumble to a stop on the sidewalk, staring up at the tower. There was silence.

Pete mumbled out of the side of his mouth, "I guess you guys did hear the bell ring."

Turn to page 45.

"**L**isten. We won't hurt you. I just hope you're not bigger than we are," said Sam, trying to use a friendly voice.

Seconds later, the door swung open slowly, and a girl's face emerged out of the shadows. The boys were all surprised, but only Sam spoke, "Hey, you're a girl!"

None of them had ever seen her before. She stepped out of the closet, but immediately shuffled aside with her back to the wall. Her arms were wrapped around herself, and she kept looking at the floor as if she were trying to find another hiding place.

"Sometimes your brilliant observations really amaze me," said Willy chuckling. "The question is, what on earth is she doing down here?"

The girl spoke very quietly, "I was just looking around."

"Was it you I saw through the leaves awhile ago?" asked Pete.

"Yes," said the girl, nodding, but still looking down. In fact, the movement of her head made her hair fall down around her face, so they couldn't see her at all.

"See?" said Pete triumphantly, "I did see someone."

Willy asked the girl how she opened the tunnel door from inside the basement.

"I don't know. I was touching a lot of things in the hall. The wood is very beautiful. The door suddenly went up—." The girl stopped abruptly, as if she suddenly realized how much she was talking to these strangers.

As he stood there watching this quiet girl, Chris was reminded of his cousin Jill, the same Jill who would be visiting for the summer. The Jill that would probably complicate his life. Maybe if he could get Jill and this girl together, they would leave him and his friends alone. . . . "What's your name?" he asked.

The girl didn't answer right away, as if her name was something she didn't give to others very easily. But then she looked up, pushed her hair back and said, "Tina."

Chris found himself acting like a fast-talking salesman. He really wanted to get this girl and Jill together. "Hi," he said. "I'm Chris and these are my friends Willy, Sam, and Pete. I also have a cousin whose name is Jill who I want you to meet. I'm sure you'll like her. Where are you from?" He sounded so silly that his friends stared at him, and the girl smiled in spite of her shyness.

Willy came to his rescue. "You will have to excuse my friend here. Sometimes his mouth gets so far ahead of his brain that the two become completely disconnected!" Chris blushed and the rest laughed. The girl put her head back down, but the boys could tell she was laughing, too.

"So, where did you come from?" Chris tried again.

"We just moved here from Brazil," said Tina.

"You mean there are more of you around here?" asked Sam.

Tina said, "My brother and I are here with my grandparents. They are going to open this church again."

"That's not going to be easy," said Willy. "This old

place has been locked up for a while. I wonder if there's anybody around anymore except Chris and me who used to come here to church. How are they going to get people to come?"

"Wait till you meet my grandfather!" For the first time the girl spoke up without a trace of shyness. "He's probably upstairs. Come on, I'll take you to meet him."

Chris said, "All right, but first, show us exactly what you touched out in the hallway. I want to find out how to open that secret door from the inside."

But even though Tina tried hard to touch the same things she had touched before, nothing worked. The sliding door never opened. It still looked like the innocent end of a hallway in the basement of an old church. That mystery would have to be solved some other time.

"Well, we've got the whole summer to work on that one," said Sam. "Let's meet Tina's grandfather."

With a growing sense of excitement they all followed Tina as she climbed the stairs to the main part of the church. They all had a feeling the events of this day were just the beginning of many adventures to come.

THE END
Turn to page 125.

"**H**ello, is anybody here?" Chris called out. No answer.

Willy was about to call again when from behind them came a familiar voice, "I'm here!" Chris and Willy jumped and whirled around. Framed in the bright light of the doorway was Jill, Chris's cousin.

"Jill, don't sneak up on us like that!" said Chris. "What are you doing here, anyway? You're not supposed to come until next week."

Jill stuck her tongue out at Chris as he was speaking. As soon as he was finished, she said, "I didn't sneak up on you—I just walked in here when I heard you yelling in the church. I can't help it if you guys scare easily. Anyway, I'm here early because Dad got a long weekend off work. They decided to bring me to Millersburg today. Is that all right?"

Chris and Jill got along pretty well, though you couldn't always tell from the way they talked to each other.

"So, what are we going to do?" Jill asked.

"What do you mean, 'we'?" asked Chris. "Willy and I were doing just fine having an adventure all on our own."

"Well, if you're going to jump every time you hear a little sound, maybe I should come along to help you not die of fright," said Jill in mock concern.

Chris realized again that he was no match for Jill in a battle of wits. He decided he would try a trick. "Jill, would you run home and get us a flashlight so we can really explore this place?"

She smiled a big smile right back at him and said, "Chris, you are hopeless. Do you think you can get rid of me that easy? No way."

Willy and Chris looked at each other. They could almost read each other's minds. Both were trying to decide whether to "lose" Jill, or let her join this adventure.

CHOICE

If you think they should find some way to avoid Jill, turn to page 60.

If you think they should let her come along, turn to page 51.

Moments later, they were back in the cool entryway, standing before the oak doors. The animal carvings were larger than life. The lamb and lion seemed to stare right through the boys.

"I was going to touch the lion a while ago, but I couldn't," Chris confessed quietly.

Jim said, "It does look like it might bite your hand off, doesn't it?"

Willy asked the question they all had on their minds. "Why did they make the doors this way, I wonder?"

A gentle voice joined their conversation, saying, "Those animals have a message for those who will pay attention."

Chris and Willy were surprised, but Jim immediately said, "Oh, hi, Grandpa. We've been studying these carvings." Out of the shadows of the basement stairway came a man whose face shocked the two boys. Chris and Willy looked at each other, speechless.

Jim said, "This is the surprise I mentioned, guys."

Willy finally stammered, "You look just like Miss Whitehead, who was our Sunday school teacher."

The man stopped, then gave a hearty laugh. "Well, I guess that makes sense. She was my twin sister! It's nice to meet someone who knew her around here. So, tell me, boys, what kind of a teacher was she?"

"She was great," said Chris.

"Yeah, she was the best!" echoed Willy.

"What do you mean about my sister being great?" asked the old man after he found out their names.

"Her classes were always fun, and she told stories," said Willy. "It seemed like no matter what happened or what we talked about, she would end up telling us a story."

The old man got a twinkle in his eyes that almost looked like tears. "You know, this lamb and lion you are looking at remind me of a lot of stories. So did the way you jumped just a minute ago when I spoke up."

The boys seemed to remember something at the same time because they all suddenly glanced at the panel that led upstairs.

The old man didn't miss those glances. "I see you've already discovered one of the secrets of the lamb," he said chuckling. The boys stared at him in amazement. "Well, what do you think I did for fun when I was a kid around here?" He lowered his voice, as if to let the boys know he would keep their secret as he added, "The stuff up there was already old when I was a kid. Explore, but be careful."

"Does the lion open any secret doors?" asked Jim.

CHOICE

Turn to page 122.

34

Willy cleared his throat extra loud. "All right, you guys," he announced, "it looks like we have a difference of opinion here. Am I right? Of course I'm right.

"So, let me say something to each of you. Pete, sometimes you are pretty stubborn. I mean, Chris and I agreed we heard a bell and saw the open door. You've gotta give us some credit. I don't think you can say Chris and I have ever lied to you on purpose, have we?"

Pete looked down for a moment, then mumbled, "I guess not."

Willy went on, "And Chris, I know you get irritated when someone doesn't believe you, but you have to admit, the door is locked and things are pretty quiet around here. Pete just likes to know what he's getting into. He's kept us out of trouble by being that way. Remember our plan to jump old man Hatcher's wall and swim in his pond that night last summer? Remember who tossed a rock over the fence to show us there were Dobermans hiding in the bushes? If it weren't for Pete, we'd have been dog food!"

Chris nodded his head thoughtfully. "You're right. Sorry, Pete."

Sam said, "Now that we got that cleared up, let's check this place out and—"

He was interrupted by the bell giving one sharp ring. The boys looked at each other with surprise, then ran down the steps to look up at the steeple. Everything was quiet again.

Pete broke the silence by saying, "Like you said, you heard the bell. Someone's in the church."

CHOICE

Turn to page 45.

"**I**f you want to check it out, go right ahead," said Willy. "I'll wait here in case you need help."

Chris was about to start down the ladder by the chimney when he thought he heard a soft groan from below. "Did you hear that?" he asked Willy.

"What was it?" replied Willy as he leaned over with the candle again and tried to look down the hole.

"I think I heard someone," said Chris. "Anybody down there?" he said louder.

"Yeah," groaned a voice from below.

"What happened?" asked Willy.

"My candle blew out and I tried to climb down here in the dark. I slipped and banged my head on the chimney. I must have gotten knocked out. I'm wedged down in this hole now and I can't go up or down. I think my arm's broken. It's numb and I can't move it. I don't even know how long I've been in here."

"It hasn't been too long," said Chris. "We heard you fall just a little bit ago. How can we help you?"

"I don't think I can get unwedged by myself. Can you climb down and pull me up?" The voice out of the darkness had an edge of desperation to it.

"I'm coming down," said Chris without hesitation. "Willy, if I get him up high enough, you can reach down and help, too. If anything happens, run for help."

There wasn't a lot of room in the shaft. Chris moved down slowly, feeling below with his foot. "What's your name?" he asked as he wondered how he was going to help.

"I'm Jim," said the voice. "Boy, am I glad you guys found me. I could have been stuck in here for a long time. You're just above me, now. Hey, what are your names?"

Willy, who was now lying on his stomach looking down into the hole said, "I'm Willy, and Chris is the one coming after you."

Having reached Jim, Chris stood on the rung above the wedged boy. He held on with one hand, bent down and began feeling around to find out how Jim was wedged in. His first discovery was a left hand reaching up to him out of the darkness. Jim had fallen back, and hit his head against the bricks of the chimney. Chris was sure he must have a terrible headache. The boy's knees were together and jammed against one of the wooden rungs. Jim's shoulders were stuck lower than his knees. He couldn't quite reach the next higher rung with his left hand.

"When I try to reach up," said Jim, "I feel like I'm gonna start falling again. My back really hurts, but I have to keep pressing or down I go."

Chris thought for a moment. "Let's try this. I'm going to put my feet as wide apart as I can. I'll reach down between my legs and pull you up until you can grab the rungs for yourself. Ready?"

"All right," said Jim, gritting his teeth.

Chris reached down and grabbed Jim's wrist with both hands. He was now leaning back against the chimney himself and he grunted painfully as the brick mortar dug into his back as he began to lift Jim's weight. As Chris pulled, Jim inched his back up until he felt as if he could lower one foot to a rung.

"Hang on," said Jim as he freed one knee and moved that foot down several inches to support himself. For that moment, Chris held most of Jim's weight. He gasped as he lost another layer of back skin against the chimney.

Jim was now able to grab the ladder rungs with his left hand. Chris climbed back up and Jim followed him slowly. When he reached the top, Willy and Chris helped him onto the attic floor.

"Thanks a lot!" exclaimed Jim. "Man, was I stuck."

Chris was proud and embarrassed at the same time. He mumbled, "That's OK. How is your arm?"

Jim moved it a little and said, "It really hurts, but I don't think it's broken. It feels like I really jammed my funny bone—which isn't very funny. My back is pretty scraped up. How's yours, Chris?"

"It hurts a little," said Chris, though it was actually stinging badly. But he sure felt good inside to have been able to help someone in trouble.

As the boys talked they decided they would wait to continue their explorations until later. Jim was obviously a new kid in town, and Willy thought it would be nice to introduce him to the Freeze.

"Nothing better than one of Betty's milk shakes after an ordeal like yours," he said with a chuckle. "Then you can tell us how you got into the church in the first place," added Willy.

THE END

Turn to page 125.

40

Pete had decided on a visit to the Freeze, so he walked down the steps and across the street heading through the Common toward the ice cream shop. As he stepped onto the sidewalk across Main Street, he suddenly froze in his tracks. The church bell sent out another clear ring.

He was ashamed he hadn't trusted his friends. He hurried back across the street and joined Chris, Willy, and Sam at the bottom of the church steps. As he approached he said, "Hey, I guess you did hear a bell. Maybe this isn't a waste of time after all. I'll try to remember to trust you next time, Chris."

CHOICE

Turn to page 45.

"It's *remember,*" Willy said quietly. "Mrs. Whitehead wrote 'Remember to be ringers' during the last class she was here."

"My great-aunt wrote that?" asked Jim as he touched the board with his fingers. His memories of his aunt were warm but very dim—mostly smiles and hugs.

But here were words that she had written two years before. He turned to Willy and asked, "What did she mean?"

"Yeah," said Sam, "what did she mean?"

Willy was staring at the words on the blackboard. He thought hard for a moment, shrugged his shoulders and said, "Beats me. I can't remember, but it seemed important to her at the time." He stopped as if trying to catch a thought passing quickly through his mind. "I got it! We never found out what she meant. At the end of every class she would always write down what we were going to talk about next week. That's why she wrote 'Remember to be Ringers' on the board. But, she didn't come to the next class because she—" He stopped because he didn't want to say again that she had died. Chris nodded his head in agreement and the group fell silent.

The awkward moment was interrupted by good old Sam with a bright idea. "Listen, guys, maybe we can figure out what she meant. If being a Ringer was something we should remember, it ought to be worth finding out what she was trying to say!"

"How can we do that?" asked Pete doubtfully.

"Let's try," said Jim. "Maybe my grandfather can help us. He's around here somewhere."

Meanwhile, Chris had been doing some thinking of his own. "I just remembered something else Miss Whitehead used to do. Whenever one of us couldn't understand a word used in the Bible or in class, she had us look it up in a big dictionary she kept right—" he pointed to a large book on a stand in the corner of the room. There it was, ready to be used.

The boys crowded around as Chris opened the cover and grabbed a thick handful of pages. He flipped to the *R* section and looked up *ringer.* Clearing his throat, he read, "Ringer, n."

Pete whispered, "That means noun."

Chris read on, "One. A person or thing that rings a bell, chime, etc." He paused for a moment.

Sam was ready with a comment. "Now see, that's what I like about dictionaries. They're so helpful."

"Hold it." Chris continued, "and Two. (a) a player, horse, etc. dishonestly entered in some competition by falsifying or concealing the facts of identity, status, age, record, etc.; (b) a person or thing that very much resembles another; as, he's a ringer for his father. Slang." He looked up at the faces looking over his shoulder.

"You lost me at the first 'etc.'," murmured Sam.

"I don't understand that one, either," said Jim, "but I don't think my great-aunt would want us to remember to be anything dishonest or false. What about that second definition, though?"

Sam pointed down at the book and asked, "What does 'resembles' mean?"

"It means you look like someone, or maybe act so much like him that other people wonder sometimes if you *are* him," said Willy.

Pete turned to Jim and said, "Sounds like your great-aunt wanted us to remember to be like someone or act like someone. Who did she want us to be like?"

As soon as he asked the question, Pete realized he knew the answer. The other boys also were pretty sure they knew the answer too. They all got a little embarrassed, the way people do sometimes when somebody asks an obvious question about Jesus. They looked at each other sheepishly.

Willy said quietly, "Miss Whitehead told us over and over that if you had to choose one person to be like, it ought to be Jesus. And I don't think she would ever be embarrassed to say it, either."

"Maybe that's why she had you read that verse on the wall all the time," added Jim. "If you really believe in someone, you should show it with your life."

"Even if you're a kid," said Willy.

Chris pointed back at the dictionary and said, "The example there says 'he is a ringer for his father.' I wonder what it would mean to be a ringer for Jesus?"

Willy started laughing, then gave Chris a little shove, "You know what you just did? You asked almost the same question Miss Whitehead always asked after we said that verse out loud. Remember how she put it? 'What will it take to make the verse be true in your life?' She'd wait a second, then say, 'You have to let Jesus make it come true in you!'" He looked at Jim, then said, still chuckling, "She always laughed when she said that, like it made her very happy just to tell us."

Jim gave a little laugh himself and said, "Wait till you meet my grandfather! He's a ringer for his sister!"

Sam couldn't miss out on the laugh so he added, "What do you say? Let's all be ringers!"

As near as the boys remembered it, that's how the Ringers got started. Four friends and a stranger exploring an old church. Little did they know that summer afternoon how many adventures were ahead of them.

THE END

Turn to page 125.

The vines and bushes around the church had been growing wild, so the boys felt like they had plunged into a jungle as they worked their way along the side of the building. The flaking white walls of the church were almost completely hidden behind a curtain of ivy leaves. Evergreens that had once been a neat hedge along the flagstone walkway had overgrown the path. There was only enough room to walk in single file. The branches could be pushed aside, but the boys soon discovered what happens when the person in front of you lets go of a branch he just pushed aside.

Pete, who was last in line, had just ducked to avoid being hit by a branch when something caught his eye in the wall of the church. Right at knee height, among the ivy leaves, he was sure he had seen a human face.

"Hey, guys," he whispered. "Stop! I just saw something!"

The other three didn't hear him right away because of the noise from the bushes. He had to take several steps to catch up with Willy. Willy then caught the attention of the others. They crowded together.

"I just saw someone watching us through the leaves back there," said Pete when he had everyone's attention. "Whoever it is must be the one who's in the church. Didn't you guys see anything when you passed that spot?" He pointed back the way they had come.

The other three shook their heads. "You sure it wasn't just the white paint shining through the leaves?" asked Sam.

"Hey, I know I gave you guys a hard time about checking out the church, but I know what I saw," said Pete. He was realizing that not trusting others sometimes leads to them not trusting you.

"OK, Pete," said Chris, "where was this face?"

"Right back here," said Pete as he turned. He struggled back through the branches, then stepped toward the church and pushed aside the ivy leaves. Behind them was only the stone foundation of the church. He stepped back and forth, trying several other spots, without luck. Realizing the others were standing watching him, he whirled around, red faced. "Listen, guys. It was around here somewhere. I'm sure of it. Help me look."

Instead, Chris, Willy, and Sam looked at each other. They could tell each of them thought this was a waste of time. Sam said, "Look, Pete, why don't we check out the back of the church, and if we don't find anything there, we'll come back and look here."

"But we're right here now," said Pete. "I know we can find something if we all look."

CHOICE ➡

If you think they should join Pete in the search for the missing face, turn to page 57.

If you think they should go on to the back of the church, turn to page 111.

Whoever was climbing down the ladder had descended two rungs when he stopped. Chris and Willy heard a boy say, "Rats!" then climb back up into the opening. The boys looked at each other and mouthed the word "rats." Chris made a grotesque face in the candlelight. As far as he was concerned, things couldn't get much worse than rats. There were some sounds that gradually faded.

"Come on, let's go after him," whispered Willy. He hadn't recognized the voice, but was curious to find out what was going on.

"What if there are rats?" Chris wanted to know.

"I'll go first," was Willy's answer.

"Well, if there's rats," whispered Chris with intensity, "I'm not coming second or third!"

As Willy started up the ladder, Chris picked up the candle from the table and handed it up to his friend. "Tell me if you see anything I don't want to see," he said.

It wasn't easy climbing the ladder holding a lit candle. Willy almost fell once. He carefully lifted the light up through the opening, then followed with his head and shoulders. "Wow," he whispered back down, "this is incredible up here! All kinds of boxes and neat stuff."

"Can you see any rats?" was Chris's concern.

"Come on up and see for yourself," said Willy in

mock daring. He climbed the rest of the way onto the landing and waited for his friend. Chris was also amazed when he stuck his head through the opening and began looking around.

In the small circle of light created by the candle he noticed the massive wooden beams reaching up into the darkness to hold the church bell. Scattered around were boxes and unusual shapes draped with cloth. Everything was covered in dust so thick you could clearly write your name in it, which was what Willy was doing at that moment.

"I wonder why we never heard about this stuff when we went to church here," said Willy, as he set a long wooden crate on the floor and tried to open it. It was nailed shut. "Remind me to bring a flashlight and a crowbar up here the next time we visit," he added.

"It'll take all summer to check out all this stuff," said Chris as he began to lift one of the covers off an odd-shaped box.

They had forgotten for a moment what had brought them up there in the first place. Now they were interrupted by a distant sound that sounded like a surprised owl. "Whooooaa!" yelled a voice that faded almost immediately in the distance, as if someone had fallen down a well. Both boys jumped in surprise.

"Now what on earth was that?" asked Chris.

"Sounded like someone ended up where they didn't want to be," answered Willy. "I think it's time to get out of here. We can get lights and stuff and come back later."

"What if he's hurt? We'd better find out," said Chris.

50

If you think Chris and Willy should leave and come back some other time, turn to page 8.

If you think they should investigate the sound, turn to page 73.

"**S**o, what can you tell me about this church?" asked Jill, interrupting and cancelling their temptation to run away. "Do you come here very often?"

"We used to come every Sunday," said Willy, "but our Sunday school teacher died, and not too long after that they closed the church. That was more than a year ago. We just happened to find the door open today."

There was a small table on the left wall of the entryway on which there was a guest book. Jill bent over and blew a large cloud of dust off the book. "This place is a mess!" she said. She opened the book and began to leaf through the pages at random. "Hmmm. This book goes back to 1930. Looks like they never had more than a page worth of visitors each year. Hey, here's your name, Chris."

The boys looked where she was pointing and sure enough, in a clumsy young man's handwriting, *Christopher R. Martin* had been recorded in March of 1940. The column "Member" had been checked, and so had the "Desire Prayer" column. In the comment space were three little words: "Off to war."

Jill said, "Chris, 1940 means World War II. This must be when Great-Grandpa Martin went to war. Mom says he was killed in France. I wonder if he imagined one of his great-grandchildren might someday read his name. I'll bet a lot of these people whose names are written here have great-grandchildren who would be interested in knowing they were here. This is like a history book."

Willy wasn't much of a fan of history. He said, "That's very interesting. We'll have to look into it sometime. Let's see if we can find out who's in the church."

"Wait," said Jill, "maybe we can find out something about your family here, Willy. We can look around later."

CHOICE ⇒

If you think they should continue to examine the book Jill found, turn to page 71.

If you think they should move on to explore the church, turn to page 64.

"E-*M-B*-blank-*R*," said Pete slowly. He repeated the letters faster, *"EMB-R, EMBER,* this part is *ember,"* he said triumphantly.

"——*ember to—ring—,"* continued Sam. "How about *November to—ring—,* or *December to—ring—,"* and with a flash of inspiration, *"December to bring your Christmas presents for Sam!"*

"You weren't even in this class, Sam," said Chris.

The boys all laughed—except Willy, who had been thoughtfully looking at the board.

"I know what the missing letters are," he said quietly, and the others turned to look at him in surprise.

CHOICE ⟹

To find out what was written on the board, turn to page 41.

The open door had created a dark corner in the room, so Willy and Chris stepped back where they thought they wouldn't be seen.

As the person climbed down the ladder, they were shocked to see that it was a boy their own age. He was a stranger. The boy kept humming and whistling like people do when they're a little scared but they don't really want to admit it, so they sing to keep the fear away.

As the boy picked up the candleholder, he began speaking to himself. "This is neat! So many places to hide and explore . . . ."

He took one step toward the door and the candlelight picked out two dim figures crouched in the corner.

"Oi!" he said as he jumped in surprise. His sudden motion blew out the candle and plunged the room in darkness. Everyone stayed absolutely still.

After a moment, the boy said with a shaking voice, "W-w-who's there?"

Willy and Chris stood up. "I'm Willy, and this here is Chris," said Willy. "We live around here. What are you doing here?"

"You guys just about scared me to death!" said the boy. Then he added, "My name is Jim, and I just moved here. Hey, do you guys have some matches? I found this candle down in the basement, but there was only one match."

"Sorry," said Chris, "we don't carry matches, either. Aren't there any lights up here?"

"I sure haven't been able to find any," said Jim.

Willy asked, "How did you get up here?"

"I guess the same way you did," responded the stranger. "I was looking at the lamb and the lion on the doors downstairs. Those two carvings are the coolest I've ever seen. Well, I touched the lamb's ear and the door swung open. I closed the door behind me 'cause I wanted to keep this place a secret."

"Willy and I used to go to church here, and we never knew about this place. Maybe it really is a secret," said Chris.

"Wait till you guys see what's upstairs. I think there are other rooms, and there are old trunks around everywhere. We'll have to get up there with some flashlights and really check it out!"

"Speaking of lights," said Willy, "don't you guys feel a little weird standing up here talking in the dark?"

"You're right," answered Jim. "I guess we'd better do something about that."

56

CHOICE ⇥

If you think they should all go downstairs and keep this room a secret for now, turn to page 75.

If you think they should go looking for some matches for the candle so they can explore, turn to page 84.

"**L**et's go for it!" yelled Chris and plunged into the vines covering the church. Sam and Willy were right on his heels. Pete turned back around with the kind of smile on his face that only comes when a friend has really made your day.

For several moments the area sounded like an elephant stampede in an old movie. The vines were moving furiously, though none of the boys could actually be seen. Then Willy suddenly stood up with a vine draped over his head and shouted, "Stop!"

"I knew it," said Pete excitedly. "What did you find?"

"I didn't find anything," answered Willy. "And I don't think we will as long as we search like this. We've got to get organized! Let's get right next to each other and work along the building together."

It sounded like a good plan, and it even worked pretty well. The vines made it hard to stay right together, though. And the boys had to get down on their hands and knees as they searched along the foundation of the church. But every time they moved aside the curtain of leaves and stems, all they found behind was the wall of rough stones. Even Pete was beginning to doubt what he had seen.

When they had looked at about twenty feet of the foundation without finding an opening of any kind, Pete decided to give up the search. He started to get up by leaning forward against the rock wall in front of him. But when he tried to push himself to stand, several large foundation blocks swung away from him and he almost went headfirst through the opening that was created. Suddenly he found himself flat on his stomach with his head in the darkness under the building.

Pete scrambled up and back in his surprise, banging his head on the top part of the opening. "Ahh," he said in agony as he staggered back rubbing his head. His companions crowded around the opening, trying to look inside. "Yes, I'm all right, except for my shattered head," said Pete when he realized the others hadn't noticed that he was in pain.

The boys quickly surrounded Pete and checked out his injuries. Sam said, "Well, there's no bleeding, but that's a nasty looking bump you got there. Look on the bright side, though. You sure proved to us you did see something."

Pete gave Sam one of those it-only-hurts-when-I-laugh looks and said, "I guess since we found it, we might as well explore this place." He was still rubbing his head gently.

"Do you want to go first?" Sam asked Pete.

"As long as I don't have to do anything else with my head," answered Pete.

He crouched in front of the opening and leaned forward, supporting himself on one hand, reaching into the darkness with the other. Under his breath he mumbled, "If something grabs me, I hope you guys can pull me out!" He felt nothing, so he moved closer until his hand was resting on the lip of the opening and his head and shoulders were in the darkness. Still nothing. He reached down along the wall below him and was surprised to discover a shelf or a step there. He reached down further and confirmed that it was a step. There was another like it below. He came back into the light and looked up at his friends. "There are stairs inside," he said with excitement. The bump on his head was forgotten.

Turn to page 119.

Chris knew he wasn't as fast a thinker as Jill, but he was pretty sure he could outrun her. He caught Willy's eye and motioned slightly toward the door. Jill had just noticed the wood carvings on the door behind the boys and was distracted for a moment. Chris and Willy bolted for the door.

They made it across the porch side by side in two leaps, and skipped the stairs altogether. Landing on the sidewalk, each tried to turn toward the other, and almost collided. Recovering, they took off in opposite directions. Chris stopped and said, "This way, Willy!" Willy spun around and followed.

At that moment, Jill burst out of the church yelling, "Chris Martin, you big goof, you're not going to get away with this!" She had seen their antics on the sidewalk and was trying not to laugh. But she didn't want to be left alone, either.

Chris and Willy shot past city hall and turned left on Maple Street. They were quickly leaving Jill behind. The boys cut left behind city hall and left again between city hall and the church, hiding behind the hedge that ran along the sidewalk. There they waited.

Jill ran after them as far as the corner. When she looked left, the boys were nowhere in sight. She was a little angry, but she was also laughing. "Chris Martin," she yelled, "I hate you!" She turned around and walked back toward the church, still talking to herself. "I'm not going to run after you all summer. If you can't be nice, I'll fix it so you have to stay home!" As she said this, she passed the hedge so close to the boys they could have reached out and almost touched her.

After Jill was gone, Chris and Willy "high fived" each other. Chris thought it had been fun to leave Jill behind. It was almost like a game of hide-and-seek, except the seeker had to keep seeking. Then he wondered why he had wanted to get rid of her. She was actually kind of fun to have around. She wasn't afraid of adventures and was pretty smart, too.

Suddenly, Chris wished he hadn't been so mean to his cousin. He would have liked to go back and start over again in the church lobby.

THE END

Chris and Willy can't go back, but you can. Turn to page 51 and read what happens when Chris includes his cousin in their adventure.

By the time Sam and Willy got to the bottom of the stairs, they could hear Pete and Chris returning. They could tell the boys were excited.

Willy whispered to Sam, "Get against the wall, and we'll jump them when they're going by us."

Pete was saying, "Those stairs must be along here somewh—!" His hand touched Willy and he froze mid-sentence.

Before he could do a thing, Willy yelled, "Boo!" Sam's "boo" was almost like an echo.

Chris was a little upset at being surprised, but he tried to act cool. "I thought you guys were going to wait for us at the top of the stairs!" he said.

"We got bored," said Sam. "So we decided to meet you. By the way, as we were coming down the stairs we managed to close the door up there. We thought we should be able to open it once you guys came back."

A cold feeling started growing in Chris's stomach. Exploring was one thing. Being trapped in a tunnel no one knew you were in was something else! "We'd better get going," he said.

Sure enough, they couldn't get the door open. They tried every trick they had learned so far. Nothing. They yelled and pounded on the door. No one came. They were running out of ideas.

In a quiet moment, Sam said, "Guys, I am really sorry I told Willy we should try to surprise you. It was a stupid idea."

Out of the darkness came Chris's voice, "Yeah, it was a stupid idea. But you couldn't have known this would happen. Usually you have pretty good ideas!"

After a while, Pete said, "I know I saw someone outside that first tunnel. I think we should keep knocking on the door and calling once in a while. Maybe that person will—" As if he had said magic words, the door opened. They could tell right away because the outside stone door was open, too, so there was light in the stairwell. They also noticed that the other door at bottom of the stairs was closed. When Willy tried the little handle they had used to lift the door earlier, it didn't budge.

Chris said, "Let's get out of here. We can come back when we're better prepared. Pete and I want to show you guys some neat stuff downstairs. We're gonna have to figure out what used to go on at this church. I'd also like to know who let us out."

"Sounds like we're in for a great summer," said Sam. "I'll try to keep from locking us in the next time." Funny how easy it is to talk about trouble when it's over.

THE END
Turn to page 125.

Willy walked over and pushed open the double doors to the sanctuary. He stopped in the doorway, with a hand on each door. He was shocked at the sight.

Just behind him, Jill put her hand to her mouth and whispered, "Oh, my!"

The sanctuary was in shambles. The pulpit, the communion table, and almost everything that wasn't bolted down had been turned over. One window along the right wall was missing, and the muddy prints around it showed that it must have been the way someone had gotten into the building. There were pop and beer cans scattered around.

The three friends walked slowly up the aisle, noting that most of the hymnbooks and Bibles that usually filled the racks behind each pew had been dumped on the floor. Some had been torn. Many of the pews had been walked on with muddy shoes.

As they came out from under the balcony that stretched across the back of the sanctuary, Willy finally said, "Who would want to trash a church?" He shook his head as if doing that might make the scene change. It didn't.

A voice from above them said, "I've been asking myself the same question."

The kids turned around and looked up. Above them,

looking down over the balcony rail, was an old man with tears on his cheeks. There was a moment of silence and then the man did something the kids never forgot. He smiled. Tears and all, he smiled. It was better than a friendly smile.

He said, "I've come up with a couple of answers to my question. Looking at this mess, my guess is that they did it because the place was empty, not because it was a church. I think they also did it because they were bored and maybe even a little scared." He turned and began to walk toward the spiral staircase that would bring him down to their level.

"But I realized something very important as I was sitting up here," he continued. "Even if I never find out who did this, I still need to clean it up and forgive them." He had reached the bottom of the stairs. He smiled again as he said, "Fortunately, none of the damage is too bad. I wonder where I might find some people to help me clean this up?"

Chris, Willy, and Jill said almost in unison, "I'll help!"

"Well, that was easy," said the old man. "The police have already been here and taken pictures and stuff, so we can get to work right away. Thanks, kids!"

Besides his friendliness, there was something else curious about this man. Both Chris and Willy noticed it right away. He reminded them of someone. They were about to ask each other when the man asked them what their names were. After they told him, he said, "I'm Pastor Leonard Whitehead. We've just moved here to open this church for God's business again."

66

"We used to have a Sunday school teacher named Miss Whitehead," said Willy.

"Ho, ho," laughed Pastor Whitehead. "So you knew my sister? Quite a lady, wasn't she?"

The boys agreed. Maybe there was hope for this church yet. This pastor seemed a lot like his sister. There was something about him that made the kids want to stick around. That Saturday afternoon flew as Jill, Chris, and Willy worked at cleaning up the sanctuary.

"We've got next week to get this ready. Then I'd like to have our first service here a week from tomorrow," said Pastor Whitehead. "My wife and our two grandchildren, who are about your age, will be helping, too," he added.

"And we've got a couple of other friends who aren't doing much this summer," said Chris. "We'll all help."

"I think there will be some interesting surprises along the way, too," said Pastor Whitehead.

The kids weren't sure what he meant, but it sounded good to them.

THE END
Turn to page 125.

"**I** still don't see why we're going down there to help this guy in the dark," said Willy as Chris began to climb down the hole by the chimney.

"Because if he's hurt down there, we can climb back up and go for help," answered Chris.

Willy waited until Chris had disappeared before he began to climb down himself. He couldn't decide whether he was following Chris because he was a friend, or because he didn't want to be left alone upstairs. The boys found that the hole was big enough for even an adult to climb down. You could only feel the chimney bricks behind you if you leaned way back.

Chris counted eighteen rungs as he descended in the dark. Where number nineteen should have been there was only space. The ladder ended.

"Willy," he called up, trying to keep calm, "we have a little problem down here."

"Now what?" said a muffled voice from above.

"There's no more ladder, but no floor either. I'm going to try to feel down with my foot," said Chris. He noticed that both of the side walls were solid, and that the chimney was still behind him. Keeping one foot on the lowest rung of the ladder he moved his hands down so he could reach down with his other foot.

Finally, his toe touched something solid.

"I guess there is a floor here after all," Chris noted as he lowered himself using just his hands. "I think a tunnel starts here—I'm sli-i-i-i-ding down! Yaaaa! Follow me, Willy!" He was gone in an instant, like a roller coaster in the dark.

"Chris," called Willy after him. "Chris! I just knew this wasn't a good idea!" He began to hurriedly follow his friend. "Even closing my eyes in this dark doesn't help!"

Meanwhile, Chris had taken a short and steep slide down some slick boards. He felt a slight bump and glimpsed an opening in front of him. Hurtling through, he crashed into a boy who was sitting on the floor of a hallway.

"What a ride!" said Chris. "That was incredible."

The boy was staring at him as if he were a ghost. "Who are you?" he asked in amazement.

In response, Chris grabbed him by the arm and pulled him aside just as the panel on the wall opened again to usher the wide-eyed, flying form of Willy, yelling at the top of his lungs, *"Look out, I'm coming through!"*

Willy rolled across the hall and landed in a heap against the far wall. "Yaww, wheee," he laughed. "Now that was a real ride! Let's go do it again." Noticing the stranger sitting with Chris, he added, "So, you're the one we've been following."

"I guess I am," said the boy. "I was just exploring this church. I sure haven't ever heard of secret doors and tunnels in a church before. See how that wood panel stays closed until you're almost down the slide before it opens? I wonder why they built it this way?"

"I don't know," chuckled Willy, "but we can sure have a lot of fun with it. Come on, let's go back up before that candle burns out."

"Who are you guys, anyway?" asked the boy as they stood up.

"I'm Chris, and this is Willy," said Chris. "We used to go to this church before it got closed. But we didn't realize there was so much to discover here. Our Sunday school class was right under this slide in that room." He pointed to a door in what he recognized as the basement of the church.

"Well, I'm Jim," said the stranger. "My grandparents are trying to get this church started again." They began walking toward the steps that would take them up to the lamb carving and its secret stairway back to the slide. "I think there must be a lot of other things to find out in this church. Let's go!" The sounds of their running feet echoed in the paneled hallway of the old basement.

For the next several hours, the boys lost themselves in using the slide. Even though the attic was dark except for the shrinking candle by the ladder hole, they learned their way through the maze of crates and shapes they would later explore. They relit the other candle and put it in the narrow room at the top of the secret stairs.

When the candles burned low, Chris and Willy suggested they all go across the Common to the Freeze for something to drink. Jim agreed, then added, "Let's keep this a secret between us, OK?"

"Right," said Chris. "But we do have a couple of

70

friends who we'll need to tell. I'm glad this church will be open again. Looks like we'll be having fun!"

Willy chimed in, "Yeah, and maybe we can find out why this building is so full of secrets!"

The boys walked out into the sunshine and ran across the Common toward the Freeze. Each was suddenly looking forward to a great summer.

THE END
Turn to page 125.

"**I** seriously doubt that my family has had much to do with this church," said Willy. "We didn't even go here until Chris and his mom invited us."

"Let's see, that would have been four or five years ago," said Jill as she flipped the pages to more recent dates. She found what she was looking for right away. "Here is where your family signed in as visitors the first time."

Willy walked over by her and sure enough there, in his dad's handwriting, was a record of his family's visit to the church.

"I remember how strange it was. Someone met us right here and told us where to go. We came for Sunday school and I got sent down to Miss Whitehead's class with Chris. I wasn't sure it was a good idea, but after I met her, I wanted to come every Sunday."

Jill bent down and tried the doors of the cabinet. They were unlocked. Inside were several other books similar to the one they had just been looking at—guest books dating back almost 150 years. There was also another small, tattered book that looked like it had been through a lot. Jill lifted it out carefully and opened the cover. She read aloud what was written on the first page, "*Our African Guests*. I wonder what this book's all about." On the other pages were lists of names and dates. Some of the dates were as early as 1820. She shook her head. "Someone wrote these names in here 170 years ago."

Chris said, "We'll have to find out what that's all about. We never heard anything about it when we were going to church here. I guess lots has happened in this old church."

Jill closed the book and gently put it back in its place. Her curiosity had been turned on. "This is one mystery I plan to solve," she said. She closed the cabinet and they moved on to other discoveries that would make this an unforgettable summer.

It was a while before they found out the reason for the book. But they stumbled on many other clues along the way. And they had many other adventures, too.

THE END
Turn to page 125.

Chris picked up the candle and held it up. The dust on the boards leading off to the left had been disturbed. "This way, Willy," he said.

They wandered between crates and shapes, following the dust prints. Twice they made wrong choices and the tracks led to dead ends, so they had to double back. As they got closer to the side of the building, they could see the roof getting lower. Ahead they spotted a brick column that Chris recognized as a chimney. And right where the bricks met the floor, they could see a black hole.

"Could he have fallen through there?" Willy wondered out loud.

"Maybe," said Chris, "if he didn't have a light."

They moved over to the opening and held the light down. Next to the hole was another candle holder with an unlit candle. Their own candle almost blew out from the strong draft. The chimney bricks formed one side of what looked like a vertical tunnel. The other three sides were made of smooth boards. But they could only see a couple of feet down the chute.

"Anybody down there?" said Chris out loud. Silence answered.

"So, what do we do now?" Willy wanted to know.

Chris tried to look down the hole again, and this time his eye caught something he had missed before. A foot

below the opening, on the side opposite the chimney
bricks, was a ladder step, almost hidden in the shadow.

"There's a way to climb down," said Chris.

Even as he said it, Willy was already shaking his head.
"I'm not going down that hole," he mumbled. "What if
something happens to us, too?"

"Well, I really want to find out what happened to that
kid, so I guess I'm going down," said Chris firmly. "You
gonna stay here, or come along?"

CHOICE ➤

If you think Willy should follow Chris down the hole, turn
to page 67.

If you think Willy should wait for Chris, turn to page 36.

Fortunately, even though the window in the stairway was very dirty, it let in enough light to help them find their way back down to the main hallway. By then, their eyes had also gotten used to the dark. After closing the secret door, the boys walked out onto the porch and sat back down on the steps. They had to squint for a while in the bright sunlight.

"Jim," said Chris, "you still haven't told us what you were doing in the church in the first place."

Jim answered, "My grandparents have a key, and they opened the building a little while ago. They're around here somewhere."

"What did they do—buy the church or something?" asked Willy.

"No, they got permission to kind of get the church going again," answered Jim.

"Well, it'll never be like the old days," said Willy. "Without Miss Whitehead it just won't be the same."

Jim looked surprised. "You knew Miss Whitehead?"

"Knew her?" said Chris. "She was our Sunday school teacher. Did you know her, too?"

"She was my great-aunt! My last name is Whitehead, too. The last time I saw her I was too young to remember, so I guess you guys know more about her than I do."

"She was really a neat lady," said Willy with some

sadness. "Being around here makes me miss her. Boy, could she tell stories. She used to get us laughing in class until our sides hurt. She made learning about the Bible a lot of fun."

Chris was a little puzzled and asked, "How come you never got to spend any time with your great-aunt? If she'd been in my family I'd have begged to visit her every chance I got."

"Well, I lived in Brazil, and we didn't travel to the States very often," answered Jim.

"You lived in Brazil?" said Willy. "That's awesome! How did you end up living in Brazil?"

"My grandparents and parents were missionaries there," answered Jim.

"You mean like out in the jungle, with the weird hats and stuff like that?" asked Willy.

"My parents and I lived in the jungle. But my grandparents lived in a big city, a lot like Washington. I usually wore a baseball cap. Do you call that a weird hat around here?" asked Jim with a playful smile.

"It depends on who the team is," said Willy laughing. Then he asked, "So, how come you're here now? Did your parents move back here?"

"No, my parents are still in Brazil," said Jim. "I'm living with my grandparents right now. They have kinda retired and moved back to the States. That way I can go to school here."

"About that strange language you were singing upstairs," asked Willy, "was that Brazilian?"

"The language is called Portuguese," said Jim.

"Sounds pretty strange and hard to me," said Willy.

"Well," said Jim laughing, "in Brazil, even the little kids can speak it!" Then he continued, "But listen, enough about my life. Let's keep exploring the church. I have a surprise to show you, too."

"All right!" said Chris and Willy at the same time.

"What do you want to do?" asked Jim.

Chris said, "Well, since I don't know how we can get a light and go back upstairs, we could just check out some other part of the church. But I was also wondering about that lion. If the lamb's ear opens the secret door, I wonder if any part of the lion's carving opens something."

"Yeah!" said Willy and Jim in chorus. Then they laughed and gave each other a shove.

CHOICE ⇒

If you think they should check out the lion carving, turn to page 32.

If you think they should go to a different part of the church and explore, turn to page 82.

"That noise came from in there," said Chris, pointing at a door that had the word "Kindergarten" stenciled on it. The boys all got very quiet. They looked at Pete.

He whispered, "I told you guys I saw someone!"

Chris led them over to the door and took hold of the handle. Sam, who was last in line again, mumbled, "Aren't you going to yell, 'We've got the place surrounded; come out with your hands up!'?"

"Shhh," whispered Willy, "You'll make me start chortling again." He could hardly say it with a straight face. They were all trying hard not to burst out laughing. All except Pete, who gave them strange looks.

Chris twisted the handle and pushed the door open to reveal a dark room. Chris found the light switch and turned on the lights. Short tables and children's chairs filled the room. Some were tipped over as if the kids had just left. A blackboard, several boxes, and an overflowing bookcase made up the rest of what was in the room. In the far corner was a storage closet with the door open a crack. If someone was in the room, it was the only place to hide.

"I saw your face outside," announced Pete loudly, "so you might as well show yourself to us." Nothing happened.

CHOICE ⇒

If you think the boys should yank open the door of the closet to find out who's in there, turn to page 107.

If you think they should give the person another chance to come out on his or her own, turn to page 27.

"**C**ome on, Pete," said Sam. "We're not in any trouble yet. If something seems the least bit wrong, I'll be all for getting out of here, too. But let's try to find out what's going on here."

Pete looked into the faces of the three boys sitting with him in the grass. All he could honestly see in their eyes was friendship. He felt the anger melting away. He really wanted to know what was going on in the church, too. There would be time later to find out if they would listen to his ideas. He got to his feet quickly and took several steps before he said over his shoulder, "Well, what are you guys waiting for?"

Surprisingly, the screen door opened without a sound. Pete led the way up the short flight of stairs to the back door, which was standing open. As they climbed, they could hear the mayor speaking. "As I said, Mrs. Whitehead, Dave and I wanted to come by and welcome you and your husband to town. The council really has wondered what to do with this old building since it was abandoned by the last members. Your letter about coming back to Millersburg and opening the church was good news. We just hope you don't get discouraged."

The boys stood just inside the back door, uncertain what to do next. There were two doors off the hallway in front of them, one on each side. The voices were coming from the one on the left. The other door was immediately on their right.

A kind woman's voice answered the mayor. "What makes you think we might get discouraged, Mr. Mayor?"

"Well," answered Mayor Johnson, "we all realize a pretty, old church is an interesting tourist attraction. But I don't think many people around here would think to go to church here."

"After fifty years in South America," said the kind voice, "I guess we've had our share of discouragements. But we have learned one thing. Behind every discouragement, God has something special plan—" She was interrupted by the crashing of the bucket Sam accidentally kicked off the landing.

CHOICE ➤

Several things may have happened in the next moments. If you think the boys were discovered, turn to page 96.

If you think the boys were not discovered, turn to page 18.

Jim told the boys there was one corner of the church he had not yet visited. There was a room to the left of the front door that he hadn't had a chance to check out yet. When they tried the door, they found it locked.

"There must be a key around here somewhere," muttered Willy. He noticed that the molding around the door stuck out quite a bit, so he suggested they check the top to find out whether a key had been placed up there. And since it was his idea, he felt that Jim and Chris should lift him high enough to reach above the door. They were willing, but almost not able. Willy wasn't light, and when you're not used to lifting someone by making a stirrup with your hands, the technique can be a little tricky.

With some grunting on his friends' part, Willy was able to hook his left hand over the molding. That steadied him. He reached his right hand into the dusty, narrow shelf created by the molding and almost immediately felt a key. In his excitement, he almost fell on his friends as he tried to get down.

It didn't take long to figure out that the bulky iron key in his hand would not fit the modern lock in the door. Nothing like a locked door in a mysterious place to raise your curiosity. But the boys had run out of ideas. What was behind that door would have to wait for another time. Willy slipped the key into his pocket and the boys decided

to turn their attention to the lion carving that seemed to
have been watching their efforts to unlock the door.

Please turn to page 32 to continue this adventure.

As they stumbled their way down the stairs, Willy had a bright idea. "Chris, doesn't Betty keep a big bowl of matches by the cash register over at the Freeze?"

"Great! I'm sure Betty will let us have some," said Chris. "And we can also introduce Jim to her."

Willy thought of something else he had been meaning to ask. "Jim, why did you ring the church bell?"

Jim chuckled. "Oh, you guys heard that? Funny thing, it was an accident. I noticed the rope when I was climbing up the ladder. Well, I slipped and almost fell. I probably would have, except I grabbed onto the rope. You should hear how that bell sounds when you're up there under it."

"It caught us by surprise out on the front steps, too," said Willy.

Closing the secret door, they walked out into the brightness of the porch. Standing on the sidewalk were Sam and Pete, Chris and Willy's best friends. The boys immediately realized they had a choice to make. Should they tell Sam and Pete what they have discovered in the church?

CHOICE ⇒

If you think they should tell the whole story right away, turn to page 93.

If you think they should keep their discovery a secret, turn to page 87.

Sam felt frantically along the wall until he rediscovered the block he had moved before.

"I guess sneaking up on Chris and Pete probably wasn't a good idea," said Willy. "Our job was to wait. But it sure is hard to be left behind!"

Just then Sam said, "Got it!" He pulled on the stone, and to his relief, he heard the door opening again. "Whew," he said. "Let's get back up there on the stairs like we never moved."

That's where they were when Pete and Chris returned from their tunnel exploration.

CHOICE ⇛

To discover what Pete and Chris found, you must turn to page 116.

If you already know what Pete and Chris found, turn to page 119 and experience a different adventure with the Ringers, or turn to page 125.

After introducing Jim to Sam and Pete, Chris announced that they had just decided to go to the Freeze for something to drink. He made a point of not mentioning their recent discoveries in the church. Pete and Sam didn't seem to notice.

"I'm always ready for a trip to the Freeze," said Sam. The boys crossed the street to cut through the park on their way to a favorite hangout.

They hadn't gone far when they heard a voice behind them calling, "Wait, Jim."

Turning, they watched an old man step briskly down the church steps and cross the street to join them. "Mind if I come along, boys?" he asked as he approached.

"Hi, Grandpa," said Jim. He introduced the old man to the boys he had just met. "This is my grandfather, Pastor Whitehead. Grandpa, Chris and Willy here used to be in Great-Aunt Millie's Sunday school class."

"Well, now that we are going to open the church again, I hope we can find someone at least a little like my sister to teach your Sunday school class," said Pastor Whitehead.

When they were seated around one of the back tables in the Freeze, the pastor had a question for them. "I'm looking for some special help with the church, and I've got a job for you boys if you're interested."

The boys looked at each other and shrugged their shoulders. "What is it?" asked Willy in a mildly suspicious tone.

The old man threw his head back and laughed, "Ho, ho, so you think the pastor might be tricking you into some hard work, huh?"

The boys were surprised he had known what they were thinking.

"It's not hard work at all," continued the pastor. "I couldn't help noticing that one of you already has found the rope to the bell. And I want you boys to ring the bell for me each time there is supposed to be a worship service at church. Would you be interested in that job?"

Willy said, "Let me get this straight. We show up early for church and yank on the bell."

"That's about it," said the pastor.

Chris chimed in, "I think we could do that." The others agreed. Pete and Sam thought their parents wouldn't mind it if they came to the church once in a while. They usually went into Washington to one of the larger churches there.

"Great," said the pastor. For him, that moment would always be the start of what became the Ringers of Millersburg. He thought for a moment, then added, "I can't pay you for your help, boys, but I'll give you a choice of gifts right now. I'll tell you a story or a riddle. You choose."

CHOICE ⇒

If you think the pastor should tell his riddle, turn to page 99.

If you think the pastor should tell his story, turn to page 102.

It only took Willy a moment to discover that the right
tunnel was actually another set of stairs going down.
Somehow, the stones that made up the stairway wall had
shifted back to reveal that the lower steps were actually
longer. They curved around to continue down. In the
darkness, there was no way to tell how far down they went.

Chris spoke up. "I'll go first this time."

"Be my guest," answered Pete.

Have you ever tried to change places on a stairway in
the dark? As always, in the middle of the confusion, Sam
had a comment. "It's been years since the last time I went
down stairs sitting down. I think I'll do this more often!"
From his companions came a chorus of boos and hisses.

Chris was about to start down when Willy had an
idea. "Listen, you guys. What'll happen if this opening
closes on us like the one we just went through?"

"Good question," chimed in Sam. "I don't think I want
to spend the rest of my summer vacation in a dark tunnel."
Though he couldn't see it, his three friends were all
nodding in agreement.

Pete said, "OK, let's have two guys go down and two
guys stay here. That way we won't all get trapped if the
door closes. I'll go with Chris. Sam and Willy, you guys
wait here. That way you can go for help if we get trapped."

They all agreed. Chris noticed his heart was beating faster. He and Pete got side by side and worked their way from step to step. Almost immediately, their faces and clothes were covered with cobwebs. "Nobody's been down here in a very long time," he said, almost to himself.

"I guess whoever I saw outside didn't come this way, then," added Pete. They had all forgotten what had started them looking for the tunnel. "They must have gone the other way," he added.

"Or a way we haven't found yet," said Sam from the darkness above them.

"Somebody remember to bring a couple of flashlights the next time we come down here," muttered Chris as he tried to pull cobwebs from his face.

Their progress was slow, but the stairs kept on going. The walls and the steps continued to be the same rough stones they had found above. Several times, the boys felt a little water seeping between the blocks.

"What's down there?" called out Sam.

"Only steps, so far," answered Pete. "I've already counted twenty-five steps. Wherever this tunnel goes, it's deep!"

No sooner had he said that than the stairs ended. By feeling around their feet, the boys discovered they were now on a level, dirt floor. They stood up carefully with their hands over their heads. They could just touch the ceiling, which was made out of rough boards.

"It's just like an old mine shaft," said Pete with excitement. "Let's keep going."

Behind them in the dark, Sam and Willy were beginning to feel left out. "The door is still open," said Sam. "How about if we join you?"

Pete and Chris were too excited to wait. "Let us check this tunnel out a little farther, then you can join us," said Chris.

"You know," muttered Sam, "they're going to leave us here sitting in the dark. Let's go after them."

CHOICE ⇒

If you think Sam and Willy should follow Pete and Chris on their own, turn to page 22.

If you think Sam and Willy should stay with the plan and wait for Pete and Chris, turn to page 116.

The boys gathered at the bottom of the steps, and Chris and Willy quickly introduced Jim to Sam and Pete. Sometimes, as soon as you meet someone, you feel like it would be easy to be his friend. That's how the boys felt about this new stranger. Jim was glad he was already meeting people his own age around Millersburg.

Willy happened to look up and see a girl come walking around the corner down by the antique shop. It was Jill, Chris's cousin. Because both her parents worked, she often spent summers with Chris's family. He started smiling when he remembered all the fun they had had last year. He was picturing how she looked when she slipped off that log at the mill pond and landed in the muck wearing her Sunday clothes. She hadn't missed a beat. Sat right there in the mud and said in a very sophisticated tone, "Oh my, and I wasn't supposed to spill anything on this dress!"

"What are you smiling about?" Chris interrupted.

"Don't look now," answered Willy, "but I see trouble coming, and her name is Jill!"

Chris couldn't resist. He looked over his shoulder, and his cousin waved at him. Jill shouted as she approached, "I've been sent by your mother to embarrass you, Chris."

"Mission accomplished!" said Chris in a friendly but mocking tone. Sometimes people who really like each other find it hard to put it into words. So they just tease each other a lot . . . like Chris and Jill.

As soon as Jill was introduced, Jim did a strange thing. He looked back at the church and said loudly, "You can come out, Tina." For a moment nothing happened, then a girl about their age appeared in the doorway. "That's my sister, Tina," said Jim. "She's homesick for Brazil, but what she really needs are some new friends." He called her down to the sidewalk and introduced her to the other five.

"So, what's happened so far this summer?" asked Jill.

Sam and Pete said in unison, "Not much." Sam added, "What'd you expect? This is only the first day!"

Jim, Willy, and Chris exchanged knowing glances. Chris said, "Listen, everybody. A lot has already happened. Willy and I were sitting here on the steps earlier when the church bell suddenly rang. We discovered the church was open, and we found a lot of other things, too. Things we would just as soon keep secret for now. We'll tell you if you can keep quiet about it until we have a chance to check it out."

"You mean like a secret club?" asked Jill.

"Well, maybe not such a big deal, but secret anyway," answered Willy.

Being the practical type, Jill suggested they needed a name to identify themselves. During the discussion that followed, someone mentioned the significance of the bell ringing. "What about the 'Ringers' for a name?" Tina volunteered quietly. Everybody agreed it sounded right. They would call themselves the Ringers.

At least, that's how some of them remembered the beginning of the gang.

Jim, Willy, and Chris proceeded to describe their discoveries so far in the old church. But before they could return for more exploration, it was time for lunch. The group agreed to meet later for more adventures.

They went on their way excited and looking forward to a great summer.

THE END

Turn to page 125 for a final word about the Ringers.

Before the boys could move, Dave Brown's head popped out of the doorway. He said, "Well, speaking of going to church, here are your first four possibilities, Mrs. Whitehead." He approached the boys, followed closely by the mayor and a smiling old woman.

Mrs. Whitehead took one look at the boys and said to the policeman, "I was kind of figuring you as one of our first possibilities, Dave." Then she said something very surprising. "Let's see, you must be William Washington." She pointed right at Willy. "Which one of you is Chris Martin?" Chris sheepishly put up his hand, like a kid who isn't sure he knows the answer to the question the teacher just asked.

"How do you know us?" asked Willy in amazement.

"Let me show you something," she answered as she went back into the room she and the two men had just left.

"You boys kind of curious about this place, huh?" said Officer Brown, not really expecting an answer.

Mrs. Whitehead returned carrying a large brown envelope from which she pulled a photograph. She handed it to Willy. The other three peeked over his shoulder. Even Dave Brown and Mayor Johnson could not resist craning their necks to see. In the photograph were three figures: younger versions of Chris and Willy, and a woman whose face lit up the whole picture.

"It's Miss Whitehead," whispered both boys.

"My sister-in-law always wrote us about the kids she knew and loved around here. You were a couple of her favorites. I wasn't sure we would meet you so soon, though," said Mrs. Whitehead. "This picture was taken not too long before she died."

Sam reached over Willy's shoulder and pointed at the picture. "What's this you guys were standing in front of?" he asked. The others looked closer. The photograph had been taken in front of a set of doors. It wasn't very clear, but just above the head of each boy, there was another face looking out of the picture.

"Oh," said Chris, "that's the inside doorway of the church. There's a lamb and lion carved on the doors. We'll have to show you sometime."

"Don't hurry," said Sam. "They almost look like you can feel their breath if you get too close to them."

"I guess this is about where I leave," said the police officer. Dave excused himself and walked toward the back door.

Mayor Johnson called to him, "Wait a moment, Dave. Sure is good to have you in town, Mrs. Whitehead. I hope the church does well." Both men left.

When the door closed, Mrs. Whitehead said, "Who are your friends here, Willy and Chris?" Sam and Pete were quickly introduced. "You'll have a chance to meet my grandchildren in a while," she continued. "I want to warn you about Tina, my granddaughter. She's quite shy. She's still not sure she likes the idea of coming to the U.S. and leaving her parents behind. Both she and Jim, my grandson, will need some good friends."

"I think it will be fun to get to know some people our age who have lived in another country," said Willy.

Mrs. Whitehead smiled and said, "That's very nice to hear. Tina and Jim sure enjoy exploring and having adventures."

"Well, then I think they will fit right in with our gang," said Chris.

And so the Ringers began to discover one another. There was much more fun to come.

THE END

Turn to page 125.

Having chosen the riddle, the five boys got quiet to listen. The old man thought for a moment, leaned forward in his chair, then began:

"An old man had three sons. He was considered a very wealthy man in the country where he lived because he had a fine herd of seventeen sheep. When he was about to die, he called in his sons and told them he had something for each of them after his death. He said, 'When I'm gone, divide up my precious herd in this way. To the oldest goes half the herd. To the next oldest goes one-third of the animals. To the youngest will go one-ninth of the herd.' Before his sons could ask him what he meant, he died. They had to solve the problem.

"The animals were so valuable none of them could be killed. How should the sons divide the herd?"

The boys were dumbfounded. None of them could think of an answer. But they agreed to keep working on it until they solved it.

THE END

Can you help the boys solve the riddle? The answer is found on page 125.

"**O**ne thing at a time," said Pete. "Let's go straight ahead." He rose to his feet and began feeling his way along the wall. Willy was holding on to his shirt, followed by Chris and Sam. Sam was shuffling his feet as he tried to keep right behind Chris. He stubbed his toe against the threshold of the door and immediately heard the door begin to slide down from above his head.

"Look out," he shouted and leaped forward. Like dominoes, his three friends piled up one on top of the other, sprawling on the floor.

"Look out?" said Chris from somewhere in the pile. "I can't see a thing."

"Hey, I'm sorry. The door was closing on me," murmured Sam.

As they were trying to untangle themselves, Willy noted that wherever they were, the floor was now carpeted.

"Yeah," said Pete, "and the walls have wood paneling on them, like they are really nice. Hey, what's this?"

Sam was about to give a sarcastic answer when there was a click and the four boys suddenly found themselves on the floor in a well-lit hallway. Pete had found a light switch. They all blinked their eyes, trying to get used to seeing.

"I know this place," Willy said. "It's the church basement. That door leads to our old Sunday school room!

I never guessed there was a secret way down here, though. I wonder why it's so well hidden?" They all looked at the end of the hallway. Where they knew there was a door, now only seemed to be wood paneling like the rest of the hallway.

"Well, I guess part of the mystery is solved," said Chris. Just then, they heard a noise.

If you think the gang is due for a surprise, turn to page 113.

If you think the gang should continue their search, turn to page 78.

The boys decided they were in the mood for a good story. Pastor Whitehead cleared his throat and began:

"I'm sure you've heard of Ecuador, one of the countries of South America. Many years ago, something happened there that changed countless lives all over the world. Sitting here with the five of you reminds me of that story. It is also the story of five friends.

"These young men, who were missionaries and pilots in Ecuador, became convinced that a tribe of Indians called the Aucas needed to be told about Jesus. But the Aucas had a very fierce reputation. They killed other Indians who lived nearby, and more than one white man who wandered into their territory had died. People had learned to leave the Aucas alone. That is, except for five young men.

"They came up with a simple plan. They would try to convince the Aucas of their friendship by dropping gifts from a plane. After months of lowering items by rope and basket from a small airplane circling the village, the men decided it was time to make direct contact. They found a river beach not too far from the Auca village, set up camp there, and waited for the Indians.

"There were several peaceful and hopeful contacts. Maybe their patient efforts had really worked. But one day the missionaries were ambushed and all five were savagely killed by Auca spears. At the time, it seemed like a terrible waste of life. Each of those young men had a wife and four of them were fathers. All of us on the mission field in many countries were stunned and sad. Many felt that the men had moved too quickly to try and make direct contact with the Aucas. Mistake or not, they had paid with their lives for their decision."

Pastor Whitehead paused for a moment, and Willy said, "Man, that really is a sad story. Why did you tell us about those guys?"

"Well, the story isn't done," continued the pastor. "Later on, the sister of one of the men who died and the wife of one of the others actually went to live among the Aucas. Eventually, many Aucas became Christians. Even some of those who had killed the young men.

"Also, many other people became convinced that God wanted them to go to foreign countries with the gospel. It was partly this story that helped Jim's dad decide to become a missionary when he was growing up."

Sam was shaking his head thoughtfully. "How could you go try to help someone after they killed your brother or your husband? That must have taken some real guts."

The pastor nodded gravely and said, "That's right Sam, though I don't think those women would agree. I think they were more concerned about how much God loves the Aucas. They knew God wanted the Aucas to learn about his forgiveness. And they wanted to forgive the Aucas, too."

After that, they had a long conversation about what forgiveness means. Pastor Whitehead was full of stories. By

104

the time the gang left the Freeze that afternoon, they all
agreed it was great to have the Whiteheads in town.

THE END

Turn to page 125.

The boys crouched in the tall weeds as two figures emerged from the evergreens. One of them was the police chief, David Brown; the other was the mayor, Mr. Johnson. They were both deep in conversation, so they didn't notice the four unusual lumps among the weeds. The two men entered the back door of the church.

Pete was the first to speak. "Let's get out of here!" he whispered harshly. His tone of voice sounded like he was daring them to take his suggestion for once.

"Are you serious?" asked Willy. "This is just starting to get interesting. Stick with us, Pete. We won't get you into trouble."

"Besides," added Chris, "we still have to go back the way we came and try to find whatever it was you saw in the vines."

At that moment, Pete had a hard time believing his friends really liked him, but they did. He just had a different way of looking at things. He was careful. Sometimes it helped. Other times, it got in the way. Right then, though, he really wasn't being careful; he just wanted the guys to agree with one of his ideas.

The boys didn't want to push Pete away. They looked at each other, trying to decide what to do.

106

CHOICE ⇒

If you think they should go along with Pete to show their friendship, turn to page 25.

If you think they should follow the two men into the church, turn to page 80.

Pete still wanted to prove to the others that he had seen a person through the leaves outside. He walked to the closet, fully planning to open the door and find whoever or whatever was in there. He never got the chance. He was still several feet from the door when it exploded open, and out shot the figure of a girl about the boys' age. She sidestepped the frozen Pete, shot between Chris and Willy, and bumped Sam on her way out the door. She was gone before they could do a thing.

"Now that's what I call movin'!" said Sam.

"Anybody recognize her?" asked Chris.

They shook their heads in unison, but Sam added, "I want *her* on *my* team."

Pete gave him a shove as he said, "I don't think you'll ever catch her to ask her."

"Oh, yeah?" answered Sam in mock challenge. He spun around and dashed out the door in hot pursuit of the girl. He was just trying to be funny again, but as he rounded the corner of the hallway, to his surprise, there sat the girl on the stairs, crying. Tears were one thing that always made Sam forget what he was going to say. He was one of those people who feels like crying whenever he saw someone else cry. He had a soft heart. "Are you hurt?" he finally asked.

The girl sniffled, wiped her tears on her shirtsleeves,

and said softly, "No." She had her head down again, and her fingers were tracing the pattern of the carpet covering the stairs.

Sam shook his head and wondered why it was that so many girls he knew seemed to cry when they weren't hurt. He decided he would try to figure it out someday. "What's your name?" he asked quietly. He didn't want to scare her.

"Tina," she answered.

"I'm Sam," he said, even though she hadn't asked. "Nice to meet you," he added because he could almost hear his mother telling him to be polite. Sam looked around himself, trying desperately to think of something else to say. He sat on the stair next to her and waited for inspiration.

Tina wiped her tears on her shirtsleeves again. She lifted her head and looked straight ahead at something or someone far beyond the church basement. Taking a slow, deep breath, she said, "I miss my parents."

"Where are they?" he asked.

"They're in Brazil. They're missionaries. My brother, Jim, and I came back to the U.S. with our grandparents. They were missionaries, too. Now we're going to live with them here in Millersburg, and they're going to open this church again," Tina explained.

"So, when will you see your mom and dad again?" asked Sam.

"Maybe next summer," said Tina looking as if she were about to cry again.

It took Sam a moment to realize what she had said.

"You won't see your parents for a whole year?" He whistled softly in amazement.

"Well, we can talk on the phone once in a while. And we can write each other. But I still miss them a lot," said Tina. She told Sam that she had agreed to come to the States with her grandparents because she really did want to find out what life was like here. "In Brazil, I went to boarding school or I did correspondence school at home," she added. Then she kind of giggled and said, "I really wanted to meet some American kids, but when that guy spotted me in the leaves out there, I got scared. I'm sorry I ran."

"Well, run is the right word for it. You are fast! The girl's track team can really use you," he said enthusiastically.

"Oh, I don't think I could do that," Tina murmured.

"We'll see," Sam responded. "Now, let's go back and find the guys and I'll introduce you." They got up and headed back toward the room.

Meanwhile, the other three had forgotten about Sam and the girl. Willy had stumbled on a pile of foam blocks in a corner of the room, and an all-out foam block war was in progress when Sam and Tina walked back into the room. "Hey," yelled Sam, "this is—." Tina, who was standing on his right, ducked, and a large block hit Sam right in the face. They instantly joined the battle. Several minutes of shouting, throwing, and ducking later, the five of them were laughing so hard they had to stop and rest. Sam was finally able to finish his sentence, "This is Tina, you guys.

Tina, that's Pete, that's Chris, and over there, laughing behind the closet door, is Mr. Take-No-Prisoners Willy."

"Hi," said Tina, trying to catch her breath. She leaned back against the wall and thought: *These guys are fun. Maybe this isn't going to be so bad after all*. Then out loud she added, "Say, do you guys know any girls my age?"

Without anybody really deciding, that afternoon Tina became part of the gang that would be known as the Ringers. Sam was right—she was a very fast runner. They all found that out when she . . . but that's an adventure to be told another time.

THE END
Turn to page 125.

"**C**ome on, Pete," said Chris. "Let's check out the back entrance." He began walking in that direction with Willy and Sam at his heels.

Pete stood there for a few moments, then grudgingly followed. He was feeling sorry for himself. *Why don't they ever agree with me about anything?* he thought to himself. He wasn't watching where he was walking and stubbed his toe on a root. The pain didn't help his attitude at all.

They reached the back corner of the church and the path became easier. The tall hedge continued on their left, like a line of burly soldiers, marching up to the gravel alley that ran behind the city hall and the antique store that stood on either side of the church. The evergreen soldiers made a sharp turn at the alley, crossed the back of the church yard, made another sharp turn at the far corner, and marched up the other side of the building.

The boys were now walking in an open space at the back of the building. Once there had been a lawn. Now, the weeds were waist high. The flagstone walk turned and led them toward the back door. A regular sidewalk went straight back from the church to the alley, though now it seemed to end at the hedge into which it disappeared.

On the back stoop, the boys noticed various lawn tools: an old hand mower and several rusty sickles. Chris was about to try the door when they all heard a car drive up and stop out in the alley. The double clap of two car doors being shut rang through the evergreens.

The boys had one of those strange moments you have as a child when you feel like hiding even though you haven't been doing anything wrong. Someone was coming. They could see the evergreens moving where the sidewalk disappeared.

CHOICE ⇒

If you think the boys should hide and see who it is, turn to page 105.

If you think they should wait in the open to find out who it is, turn to page 12.

Before the boys could move out of the way, a panel in the wall next to them slid up, and out hurtled the form of a boy, yelling, "Woooooh!" He touched down on the carpet, rolled once, and landed on top of Willy. "Man, was that an incredible ride!" he said loudly, to no one in particular. It seemed to take him a moment to realize he was surrounded by boys his own age who were staring at him.

The others were dumbfounded. As usual, Sam was the first to find something to say, "Hey, who are you, and where did you come from?"

"My name is Jim," the boy answered, "and I come from Brazil."

"You mean, somewhere behind that wall is Brazil?" asked Sam, smiling.

"Oh, that," said the boy smiling back, "I'll have to show you what's behind that wall. I meant that I just moved here from Brazil."

The boys quickly discovered that this newcomer was part of a family that was reopening the church. Not only was he the boys' age, his last name was also Whitehead, the name of Chris and Willy's favorite Sunday school teacher who had died over a year before.

"So you knew my great-aunt," said Jim shaking his head in amazement.

"Knew her?" exclaimed Willy. "We loved her! She was

really a neat lady. Our class used to meet every Sunday in that room right there." He pointed to one of the closed doors along the hallway. Jim got up, walked over, and opened the door. He reached in and turned on the light. The other four got up and followed him into the room.

"Hey," said Chris softly, "they left it just the way Miss Whitehead had it."

On the wall opposite the door, stenciled in neat letters above a well-worn blackboard, were three lines Chris and Willy knew by heart. Jim read them out loud: "Don't let anyone look down on you because you're young . . . be an example to them of what a real believer is like . . . in words and actions; love, faith, purity."

"Your great-aunt had us say those words every week," said Willy as if he were looking back at a good memory. "They come from the Bible," he added.

"I know," said Jim. "My grandfather taught them to me a long time ago."

"Yeah," Chris chimed in, "and she always asked us afterwards to tell her how these words could become true in our lives."

"So, what did you tell her?" asked Sam curiously.

"The first time she asked me, I had to tell her I didn't know," said Willy remembering something else that meant a lot to him. "She asked me if I wanted to know, and when I told her yes," he continued, "she told me I needed to trust Jesus to make me into that kind of person, that it wasn't something you could just do on your own." His voice cracked like he might start crying. The other boys looked down, embarrassed.

While Willy was talking, Jim had walked around the old table and chairs to stand by the blackboard. Now he broke the silence with a question, "Can you guys see what's written here?"

The others gathered around him. There were some legible letters at the top of the blackboard. The rest had been erased. Pete spelled the letters that were plain. "There's a long blank, then *E-M-B*, small blank, *R*, blank, *T-O*, longer blank, *R-I-N-G*, blank. This is just like the TV show!" he said, getting excited. "Who wants to guess the missing letters?"

CHOICE ⇒

If you think you can figure out the message, turn to page 41.

If you can't figure out the message, turn to page 53.

Willy shook his head. "I don't think we should go after them till they tell us to, Sam. We're supposed to be the backup." Sam knew his friend was right even if he didn't want to admit it.

"OK," he said, grumbling. "But they'd better hurry up."

Meanwhile, down in the tunnel, Pete and Chris were carefully walking forward. They were side by side with their arms stretched out in front of them. They had taken a few shuffling steps when Chris felt Pete suddenly lean hard against him, forcing him to bump the side of the tunnel. "Hey, Peter," he said, "You're pushing me against the wall!"

"No I'm not," mumbled Pete. "This tunnel is getting narrower."

The tunnel took a sharp right turn. "We're going away from the church now," observed Pete. Several steps and then another right turn. "Now we're headed for the Leap!" he added in his best travel agent voice. He was referring to a steep drop-off down beyond Pine Street.

Shortly after that, a door blocked their way. They were becoming experts at examining doors and immediately began feeling around in the dark. Apparently, this was a normal door. Chris took the handle and opened it. The rusty hinges screamed as the heavy door slowly swung open.

"Well, what do you know . . ." said Pete as he felt his

way through the doorway. "I think I just found some old matches." There was a scraping sound and a small shower of sparks, and a little flame burst from Pete's hand and flooded the space with light.

Ahead of them the boys saw a room dug out of the earth. There were several cots with rumpled covers as if someone had slept in them the night before. But judging by the layers of dust, there was no doubt these beds had been unused for years.

"Ouch!" said Pete as the first match burned down to his fingers. He lit another and said, "I've only got two more. We'll have to come back and check this out some other time." They discovered another door across the room, but this one they couldn't budge. They had closed the door they came through and started back toward Willy and Sam when they used up the last match.

Pete told Chris to stop. "Why would somebody want to sleep and hide way down here out of sight under the church?" he asked. "Did the church people know what was going on down here?"

"You're sure full of questions," Chris said, chuckling.

"Well, you have to admit this church creates a lot of questions, don't you?" came Pete's answer out of the darkness.

"So," said Chris, "our task will be to figure out why an old church would have tunnels and secret passageways. But we want to keep them a secret if we can. Sounds like real detective work to me."

They groped their way back to the others to continue on their adventure.

118

THE END
Turn to page 125.

Feetfirst, Pete worked his way over the lip of the opening and down the steps. The others followed. All that could be heard was the sound of dirt and pebbles hitting the steps as the boys slid their way down. For some reason, the noise and the excitement made Sam start laughing. He tried to hold back. It was like the muffled giggling that happens when parents tell their kids to be quiet late at night. But Sam had started an instant chain reaction. Other little grunts of strangled laughter were heard. Out of the darkness below came Pete's harsh and strained whisper, "Will you guys quit chortling!"

It was the wrong thing to say. Sam tried to repeat the last word Pete had used. "Chortl—?" was all he got out before bursting into uncontrollable laughter. Willy and Chris couldn't contain themselves either.

"What's 'chortling'?" whispered Chris after several moments of laughter accompanied by Pete's attempts to quiet the outburst.

"It's what you guys were doing. Now be quiet, will you?" answered Pete in an angry whisper. There was a moment of silence, then he added in a different tone, "There's a door at the bottom of the stairs."

By the time the others had slid down around him, he had another announcement. "I can't find a handle. What do we do now?"

Willy said, "Listen guys, if one doorway is made out of rocks that move, then this doorway must have something special about it, too. What other ways can a door open?" They tried pushing with no result. Sliding the door left or right didn't work either. They felt the walls on each side of the stairs to check for hidden latches or buttons. The door didn't budge.

There was a silent moment of frustration. Then Sam asked softly, "Anybody got a garage door opener?"

Chris chuckled, but Willy exclaimed, "Hey, that may be it." He leaned over and felt along the bottom of the door. Almost immediately his fingers found a small loop of metal. He grabbed it and pulled. Silently, the door began to rise. "It's opening!" he said, even though the others already knew it by the flow of cold air coming out from under the door. "It must have weights on pulleys like the windows in my grandmother's old house," Willy said to no one in particular. His loud whisper echoed in the open space before them.

Along with the echo of his voice, Willy thought he heard another sound that had begun when the first door stopped rising. A soft, creaking noise to his right. He reached out in that direction only to discover that the wall that had just been there was now gone. There wasn't one opening, there were two, as if when the first door was opened it automatically opened a second door. All of this, of course happened in less than a moment. Willy tried not to shout out his excitement. "You're not gonna believe this! There's two ways to go!"

"What?" whispered the others almost in unison.

"There's another tunnel on my right," said Willy.

Quickly, so quickly that Willy almost got pushed through, the boys all leaned that way to feel the opening. "Hey, slow down," Willy said. Then he added, "Which way do you guys want to go?"

Almost as if in answer to his question, the boys heard another sound, this time behind them. Sam, who was highest on the steps, twisted around just in time to see the rocks that had let them into the stairway grind shut. Their eyes had gotten used to the dim light from outside, but now there was complete darkness. In the shocked silence that followed, Sam said softly, "Well, one way we can't go is back!"

CHOICE ⇒

Two dark tunnels. Which way should they go? If you decide they should go to the right, turn to page 90.

If you decide they should go straight ahead, turn to page 100.

The old man thought for a moment, then answered, "Yes, but not in a way you would expect. I think for now you better find out all you can with your discoveries upstairs. The lion will be better later. I agree with what Willy said a while ago. The lion is scary to touch. You need to understand more first."

The boys really didn't understand, but in a way they were happy to wait until some other time to discover the secrets of the lion.

"Would you mind telling us one of those stories you mentioned?" asked Willy.

"Well, let me put it to you this way," said Grandpa Whitehead, "being in the middle of things can be confusing and frightening. You look at these doors and you have questions. You wonder why the lamb and lion were carved on them. You wonder why the lion is scary. I've even known a few people to say that the lamb is scary, too. They didn't like the way it looked at them.

"But when you understand more, these carvings will look different. You may not know everything, but you'll understand better. The lion may always be scary, but someday, I hope the carving will scare you in a good way.

"One of the best ways God has helped me throughout my life is by reminding me that he always understands better, and has everything under control.

"You know, there are a lot of places in the world where people have never seen a white person, or even a black person for that matter, Willy. But people in our country have given tons and tons of used clothes away that have ended up in the strangest corners of the world.

"A missionary had an unexpected experience not too long ago in the jungles of Irian Jaya. She was walking along a remote trail in the jungle when she heard some rustling among the vines and thick underbrush next to the pathway. Stopping to discover what it might be, she called out a greeting in the local language. All of a sudden, a fierce-looking warrior covered with paint and wearing a grotesque mask sprang out of the bushes. He rushed toward the woman, shouting and waving a deadly spear. The menacing screams had a strange eerie echo behind the mask. It was a nightmare in broad daylight."

The old man paused and looked at the boys, who were leaning forward in attention to the story. They couldn't stand the suspense. Willy said, "That's it, that's the same thing Miss Whitehead used to do. She'd get us going on a story, then stop right in the middle of it. What happened to the woman?"

Jim's grandfather continued, "Well, later, the missionary confessed she would have probably fainted from fear except for one thing. The warrior was also wearing an old T-shirt that must have been part of a goodwill bundle given to his tribe. On the front was the picture of a child, and the words: 'Please be patient, God is not finished with me yet!'"

The boys burst out laughing.

After letting them enjoy the humor for a moment, the pastor continued, "You will have plenty of frightening and confusing experiences in life. But if you watch carefully, you will also find that every situation also has clues that show you God is involved. When you can't know everything, it helps to trust someone who does.

"And as far as the story is concerned, as soon as the warrior realized this woman wasn't about to strike back with magic or weapons, he became a perfect host and led her into his village.

"Now, I'm about ready for a break, and if I remember correctly, Betty Metz makes a great lemonade over at the Freeze. Can I buy you boys some refreshments?"

He didn't have to ask twice. Even the best adventures include a break once in a while.

THE END

The Ringer adventures have just begun.

Their discoveries in the mysterious old church have given them many clues and questions they will have to figure out. You might even be curious about what they have found. There are new discoveries to make. It will be a busy summer for them.

Make sure you haven't missed any parts of the adventures in this first collection, and look for others to follow. Get to know Chris, Willy, Jill, Jim, Tina, Sam, and Pete. You may even decide to become a Ringer, too.

THE END

By the way, here's the answer to Pastor Whitehead's riddle:

The boys invented an invisible sheep and added it to the herd. That way, they had eighteen sheep in the herd. Now use the farmer's directions and you will find that the total of one-half, one-third, and one-ninth of eighteen, when added together, equal seventeen. But we hope you figured that out on your own.

Neil Wilson is a contributor to the *Life Application Bible* and has authored several of the award-winning *Life Application Bible Studies*. He has also written curriculum for senior high and junior high young people.